Myths and Legends

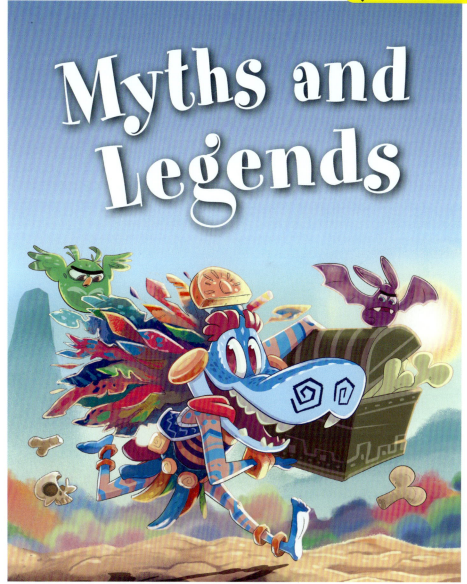

Edited by Seth Rogers

Publishing Credits

Rachelle Cracchiolo, M.S.Ed., *Publisher*
Conni Medina, M.A.Ed., *Editor in Chief*
Nika Fabienke, Ed.D., *Content Director*
Véronique Bos, *Creative Director*
Shaun N. Bernadou, *Art Director*
Seth Rogers, *Editor*
Valerie Morales, *Associate Editor*
Kevin Pham, *Graphic Designer*

Library of Congress Cataloging-in-Publication Data

Names: Rogers, Seth, editor.
Title: Myths and legends / edited by Seth Rogers.
Description: Huntington Beach, CA : Teacher Created Materials, [2020] |
  Includes book club questions. | Audience: Age 13. | Audience: Grades
  4-6. | Summary: "Action! Adventure! Romance! From Greek and Aztec gods
  to Irish giants and Chinese zodiac animals, this collection of myths and
  legends from around the world has it all!"-- Provided by publisher.
Identifiers: LCCN 2019031465 (print) | LCCN 2019031466 (ebook) | ISBN
  9781644913529 (paperback) | ISBN 9781644914427 (ebook)
Subjects: LCSH: Readers (Elementary) | Tales.
Classification: LCC PE1119 .M98 2020 (print) | LCC PE1119 (ebook) | DDC
  428.6/2--dc23
LC record available at https://lccn.loc.gov/2019031465
LC ebook record available at https://lccn.loc.gov/2019031466

Image Credits

Illustrated by: Front cover, p.1, p.14–17 Guille Rancel; pp.4–8 Daniel Shaffer; pp.9–13 Tim Paul; pp.18–22 Conrad Roset; pp.23–27
Meimo Siwaporn; pp.28–31 Fermin Solis. Courtesy Luma Creative Limited. All rights reserved.

5301 Oceanus Drive
Huntington Beach, CA 92649-1030
www.tcmpub.com

ISBN 978-1-6449-1352-9

Table of Contents

The Golden Staff

Long ago, at the dawn of time, the most powerful god of all, Viracocha, fashioned the first people of South America from clay.

Though he gave them voices and crops to harvest, the people had no skills. They didn't know how to make clothes or build houses. They couldn't read, write, or cook. So, for a long time, they lived like animals.

The sun god, Inti, looked down on the people, and he felt pity for them. He decided that the cleverest of his four sons and his daughter should rule over everyone and teach them how to live in a better way.

Their names were Manco Cápac and Mama Ocllo.

"Teach them how to live together, and help them to build a great civilization," he told his children. "Be a father and mother to them all."

And he handed them a magical golden staff that shone like the sun.

"On your travels, you will find a place where this golden staff sinks deep into the ground with just one blow. There, you must build a great city. This place will be the center of your empire and home to a magnificent sun temple. It is there that the people can come and worship me," said Inti.

As the sun rose the next morning, Inti took Manco Cápac and Mama Ocllo to the Isla del Sol, an island in the center of Lake Titicaca in Bolivia, where he was born. "Begin your journey here, my children."

However, Manco Cápac and Mama Ocllo didn't realize their three brothers were deeply jealous of the important task they had been given. They wanted to rule the new empire all by themselves. Just as Manco Cápac and Mama Ocllo set out on their journey, the brothers stepped out of a nearby cave.

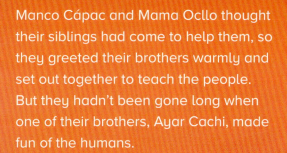

Manco Cápac and Mama Ocllo thought their siblings had come to help them, so they greeted their brothers warmly and set out together to teach the people. But they hadn't been gone long when one of their brothers, Ayar Cachi, made fun of the humans.

"What idiots!" he sneered. "Look at them. Who would want to teach such dumb beasts? What a waste of my powers! I can knock down hills with a single shot of my sling—and that's far more fun than hanging around with these fools!" And Ayar Cachi destroyed a hill with his slingshot, injuring the people who lived there.

Manco Cápac was so angered by his brother's foolishness and destruction, he used his powers to send Ayar Cachi back to the cave where he came from and sealed him inside.

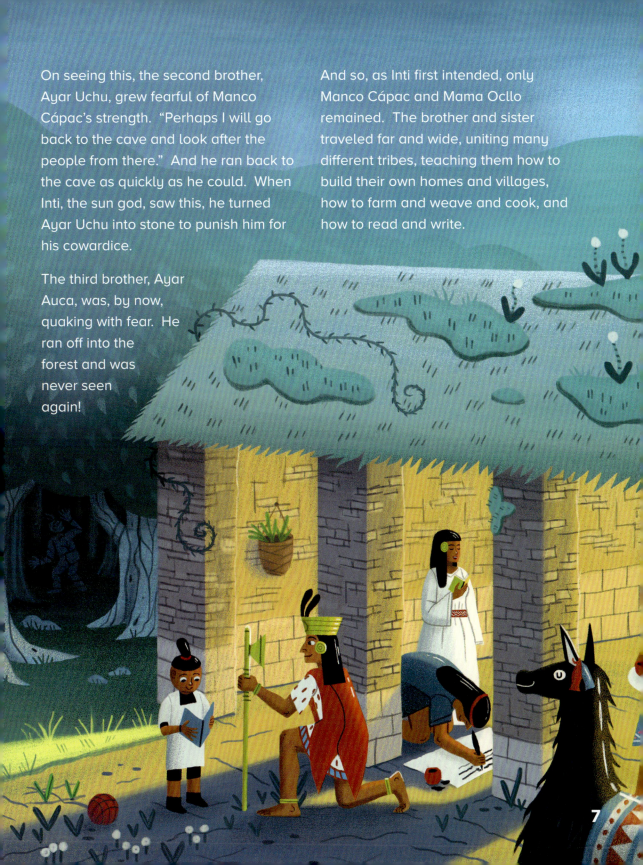

On seeing this, the second brother, Ayar Uchu, grew fearful of Manco Cápac's strength. "Perhaps I will go back to the cave and look after the people from there." And he ran back to the cave as quickly as he could. When Inti, the sun god, saw this, he turned Ayar Uchu into stone to punish him for his cowardice.

The third brother, Ayar Auca, was, by now, quaking with fear. He ran off into the forest and was never seen again!

And so, as Inti first intended, only Manco Cápac and Mama Ocllo remained. The brother and sister traveled far and wide, uniting many different tribes, teaching them how to build their own homes and villages, how to farm and weave and cook, and how to read and write.

A great civilization grew around them, and the people loved their leaders.

After many years of traveling and teaching, they reached a place called Cusco in a river valley in Peru. Manco Cápac tried to drive the golden staff into the soil. He had tried many times before, but this time found that it sank into the ground with great ease.

In an instant, a stunning temple to the sun god, Inti, sprang up before them. It had walls of glittering gold and a courtyard filled with golden statues.

Inside, there was a golden wall with a spectacular carving of the sun, which lit up the whole temple. They called the temple the Sun House.

With Inti's temple in place, Manco Cápac and Mama Ocllo set to work building a great city around it and a palace for themselves. From there, they ruled over the city they had created and all the people around it. And that is how the Inca empire came to be. 🌀

Finn MacCool

Hundreds of years ago, the northern part of Ireland was home to a giant known as Finn MacCool. Despite his large size and huge strength, MacCool was a kindly giant, who enjoyed living peacefully with his wife, Oonagh.

However, he had one great rival who lived across the sea in Scotland—his name was Benandonner, the Red Man. Benandonner spent all day and night shouting insults across the waves at Finn MacCool until, one morning, MacCool decided he could take no more. He broke off some rocks and started throwing them into the sea to build a pathway across the sea to Scotland. When he had finished, he was quite exhausted, but he yelled at Benandonner to come to Ireland and fight him once and for all.

However, when mighty Finn MacCool caught sight of Benandonner in the distance, he realized that the Scottish giant was twice his size!

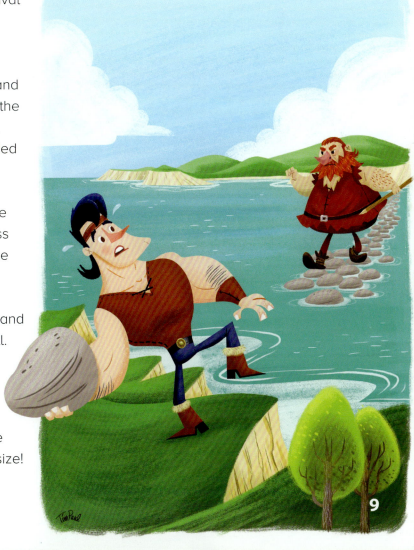

Though MacCool could easily fit 50 men in his hands, Benandonner looked like he could lift a hundred or more! MacCool regretted picking a fight, and he ran home to his clever wife, Oonagh, who always knew what to do.

"Quick as you like, now," she urged her husband. "Go and tear down two trees and fetch your ax, some nails, and your hammer!"

MacCool dashed outside and tore two trees out of the hillside, then he presented them to Oonagh. "Now, carve a sharp point in the end of one tree, and cut the other tree into long planks. When you've finished, lean the pointed tree against the wall, and nail the planks to our bed to look like a cradle."

MacCool was puzzled, but he knew it was wise to do as his wife said.

"Right, get into the bed now, and I'll wrap the blankets around you and a sheet around your head. You need to pretend you're a baby!"

MacCool curled up in the cradle and

sucked his thumb. "Close your eyes," Oonagh told him, "and when you hear Benandonner sit down, let out a wail!"

Soon enough, Finn MacCool heard the thumping steps of Benandonner coming toward his fort, followed by the thud of a heavy fist on the door.

Oonagh opened the door and said in a stern voice, "There's no need to bang so hard! You'll wake the baby! If it's Finn you're after, then he's out hunting, but you can come in and wait if you like."

Benandonner entered the great hall, and Oonagh said, "Would you like to put your spear next to my husband's?"

She pointed at the tree with the sharp end, and Benandonner was startled to see its size. He put his smaller spear right next to it, then sat down heavily on the bench, nervously crushing a boulder between his fingers. At this, Finn MacCool wailed like a baby.

"Oh dear," said Oonagh. "The baby must be hungry. I've made some pancakes. Would you like some?"

"Irish giants are famous for their extra-strong teeth."

Benandonner accepted, but when he bit down on his pancake, he chipped his two front teeth because Oonagh had hidden an iron disc in it!

"Whatever's wrong with you?" she exclaimed. "Why, my husband eats these all the time. Even the baby eats them!" She gave Finn, disguised as a baby, a pancake without an iron disc hidden inside. Benandonner saw the baby eat it without any trouble, and he started to feel most worried.

"Sure enough," said Oonagh. "Irish giants are famous for their extra-strong teeth. Didn't you know? You should come over here and have a feel of them!"

Benandonner approached the cradle and, when he saw the giant size of the baby in it, he was horrified. He cautiously put his finger by the baby's mouth to feel its teeth, and Finn MacCool bit down on it as hard as he could.

Benandonner jumped back, roaring in pain. *Goodness* he thought. *If the baby is this big and strong, how gigantic must his father be?*

Terrified at the idea of fighting the baby's father, he made his excuses to Oonagh and dashed out the door, taking giant strides as he went. Finn MacCool threw off his baby disguise, leapt out of his cradle, and did a merry dance with Oonagh!

Benandonner, the Red Man, bounded all the way home to Scotland, kicking over the rocks in Finn MacCool's path as he went. Lucky MacCool was never tormented by the Scottish giant again—and it was all thanks to his clever wife, Oonagh, who had brains just as her husband had strength. 🌀

The Feathered Serpent God

Quetzalcoatl, the feathered serpent god, was different than the other Aztec gods. He was a good and caring leader who didn't believe in sacrifice.

Perhaps this was because it was Quetzalcoatl who brought people to life in the first place. You see, at the dawn of this world, there were no men, women, or children. This made Quetzalcoatl sad, so he decided to travel to Mictlan, which was the Aztec name for the underworld, to find the bones of the people who had lived long, long ago and bring them back to life again.

He asked his twin brother, the dog-headed god Xolotl, to guide him. "The Lord and Lady of the underworld won't give up their bones easily," Quetzalcoatl warned him, but Xolotl was happy to help.

Xolotl led the way, using his amazing sense of smell to find a route through the underworld passages until they reached the Lord and Lady of Mictlan. They were sitting on thrones made from skeletons, with bats and owls perched beside them. They wore bone jewelry, and around them, old chests overflowed with yet more bones.

Quetzalcoatl greeted them politely. "With your permission, I have come for the bones of the ancient people, so I can bring life to the world again."

The Lord of Mictlan was irritated. It was law that he couldn't refuse a request from a god, but he didn't want to give up his collection of precious bones.

"You can have the bones if you can entertain me with this instrument," he sneered, handing Quetzalcoatl a conch shell with no hole in it. It would be impossible to make music with it.

"No problem," said Quetzalcoatl. "Let me go and compose a tune for you."

Xolotl thought they would have to give up, but Quetzalcoatl had a plan. He left the Lord and Lady's chamber, then summoned worms and asked them to gnaw holes in the shell. Next, he called for bees and asked them to buzz inside the shell.

When Quetzalcoatl returned, he put his mouth to the shell, and it hummed and buzzed a tuneful melody. The Lord and Lady scowled. "Now, may I have some of your bones, please?" asked Quetzalcoatl.

"Very well," said the Lady of Mictlan. "But only if you promise they will be returned to us one day."

"Of course," agreed Quetzalcoatl. "Humans are mortal, so you will get your precious bones back."

"OK, take some," she sighed. Quetzalcoatl opened up a large chest. He and his brother grabbed as many bones as they could carry.

But they hadn't gone far when the Lord and Lady of Mictlan began to have doubts. "Stop! We've changed our minds. Bring our bones back!"

Quetzalcoatl turned to his brother. "You're faster than I am. Drop your bones and run back to the chamber. Tell the Lord and Lady I will leave the bones here. Delay them as much as you can so I can escape."

Xolotl did as his brother asked, but the Lord and Lady of Mictlan saw through his lies. They chased after him, and when they discovered that Quetzalcoatl

hadn't dropped the bones, they sent their bats and owls to bring him back.

They also used their powers to make a deep hole in his path. The feathered serpent god was running so fast, he couldn't stop. He fell headfirst into the hole, breaking many of the bones he was carrying.

When Xolotl caught up with him, he leapt into the bottom of the pit and hauled his brother out.

Together, with owls and bats flapping and pecking around their heads, they ran as fast as they could. At last, they managed to outrun the Lord and Lady of the underworld and escaped into the bright sunshine.

Quetzalcoatl wasted no time. The next day, he brought humans back to life.

For a long time afterward, the Aztec people believed that humans came in different shapes and sizes because they were fashioned from the broken bones Quetzalcoatl had brought with him from Mictlan.

Persephone
and the Seasons

It was a wonderful day. The sun's rays were beating down on the lush green meadows, and the sound of laughter was ringing across the hillside. It came from the beautiful young maiden Persephone, who spent many carefree afternoons there.

Persephone was the daughter of the great god Zeus and Demeter, the goddess of nature. She was the goddess of spring flowers, and wherever she walked, no matter how bare the earth, it blossomed beneath her feet.

Persephone was worshipped and adored by all who met her because of the joy and beauty she brought to people's lives. Persephone's own mother, Demeter, thought she was so precious that no god or man would ever be good enough for her daughter. Demeter always made sure that any suitors were quickly sent away.

However, one suitor was determined not to be frightened off. He was Hades, god of the Underworld. As one of the most powerful gods, Hades was used to getting his way, and he had fallen deeply in love with Persephone. When Demeter refused to let him marry her daughter, Hades decided to do things his own way.

One day, as Persephone gathered a posy of flowers for her mother, she noticed a radiant and lovely flower she had never seen before. It was an enchanted narcissus, and as she reached down to pluck it, the earth ripped in two and a great crack appeared.

Zeus heard Demeter's threat, and he knew that the humans would not survive. Because Persephone had eaten six seeds from the pomegranate, she should spend six months of the year with Hades in the Underworld and the other six months on Earth with Demeter. Persephone was delighted at this idea.

Every spring, Persephone leaves the Underworld. Demeter's joy at seeing her daughter causes Earth to spring to life again. Persephone spreads spring buds and blossoms wherever she goes, and Demeter makes the crops grow and the fruits ripen. Later in the year, Persephone returns to Hades in the Underworld. This causes the flowers to fade and the leaves to fall, bringing on autumn and winter.

According to Greek legend, this is how the seasons came to be.

The Emperor's Race

Long ago, the Jade Emperor who lived in the heavens and ruled over China decided to challenge all the animals to a race.

"The first twelve animals to cross the raging river and reach me will be forever remembered as a sign of the Chinese zodiac," he announced. "Each animal will represent a different year."

When the cat heard about the race, she felt sure she would win. She boasted about it to her neighbor, the rat, whom she often teased and bullied.

"Of course I will be the first and most important animal in the zodiac," she purred. "The Emperor would never welcome a smelly little rat like you."

But on the morning of the race, the rat got his revenge. As the cat slept soundly, curled up in a ball, the rat snuck away to the river and didn't wake her up.

By the time the cat arose, it was too late. She had missed the race. They say cats have never forgiven rats for this deed, and that's why they still chase them today!

When the rat reached the riverbank, there were eleven more animals lined up and ready to race. There was a big brown horse, a small goat, a slow pig, a slippery snake, a fierce tiger, a fire-breathing dragon, a strong ox, a lively rabbit, an excited dog, a crowing rooster, and a fidgety monkey.

The Jade Emperor signaled the start of the race, and the animals leapt into the freezing water. The current was so strong, the little rat was swept down the river. No matter how much he struggled, he couldn't move forward. The water sent him crashing into the side of the strong ox. Seeing his opportunity, the rat grabbed the ox's tail and scrambled onto his back.

The strong ox powered through the water with ease and was the first to reach the other side of the river. He thundered toward the finish line, sure that he would finish first. However, seconds before he reached it, the rat leapt from his shoulder and scurried over the line. The cunning rat became the first sign of the Chinese zodiac, and the ox was second.

"Congratulations, rat!" cried the Jade Emperor, clapping loudly.

Just behind them, pounding over the line, came the fierce tiger. She was an excellent swimmer, but her heavy fur had slowed her down, and she roared with disappointment.

To the Jade Emperor's surprise, the lively rabbit came fourth. She had cleverly made her way across the rapids by daintily hopping from one rock to another. As she bounced over the finish line, the other animals let out a big cheer.

Next came the fire-breathing dragon. The Jade Emperor was puzzled.

He had expected the dragon to come first, as he was the only animal in the race who could fly.

As the dragon soared across the line, he said, "I am sorry to be late, Jade Emperor. I heard cries for help as the race began, and rushed to assist some nearby villagers."

This was the nature of the dragon, so the Jade Emperor thanked him.

Moments later, the big brown horse galloped toward them, shaking the water from his mane. However, when he was just meters away from the finish line, he bucked. The slippery snake slithered around his feet and rushed ahead, coming in sixth place.

Close behind the snake and the horse was an unlikely trio of friends—the little goat, the fidgety monkey, and the crowing rooster. Fearing they would never get across the river, the three had worked together to build a raft.

The little goat's horns had been so useful for nudging the heavy raft into the river that his two friends decided that he should cross the line first.

The rooster let the monkey go ahead of him, so he was the last of the trio.

Just as the rooster crossed the line, the excited dog came padding across the field looking happy with herself.

"I thought you would get here sooner," said the Jade Emperor.

"Yes, but there were so many new and interesting scents to sniff, I forgot I was in a race!" said the dog.

The Jade Emperor laughed and patted the dog.

There was a long wait before the slow pig finally crossed the line, squealing and oinking all the way.

It turned out that she had stopped to graze on the riverbank and had taken a quick nap!

And so, the Emperor's great race was over, and the pig became the twelfth and final animal in the Chinese zodiac. Everyone cheered!

From that day on, the 12 animals took turns guarding the gates of the Jade Emperor's heavenly home. They each look after a different year of the Chinese zodiac, bringing good fortune and surprises. 🌀

The Salmon of Knowledge

When the giant Finn MacCool was just a wee lad, his family sent him away to be educated by old Finnegas, the wisest man in all of Ireland.

Finnegas lived by the banks of a pool with cool crystal waters, which lay right next to the River Boyne. For seven long years, Finnegas had been trying to hook one particularly special fish there. This fish was the magical Salmon of Knowledge, and local legend said that just one bite of the fish would give the person who caught it all the wisdom in the world.

However, no matter how many hours Finnegas fished, day or night, he could not catch the slippery character.

When Finn MacCool arrived at Finnegas's little house, the old man was pleased to have some company at last and was delighted to share all that he had learned. The two got along well, and Finn was a keen learner.

One day, as they sat at the edge of the pool with Finnegas teaching young Finn MacCool how to write poetry, a glorious flash of silver caught the old man's eye. He leapt to his feet. "That's it! I know it is. Seven long years and, at last, it's here! It's the Salmon of Knowledge!" he cried.

Finn looked into the pool, and indeed, he saw a giant salmon streaking through the water like mercury. Finnegas quickly snatched his strongest net and dropped it into the pool. He splashed about, trying to haul in the colossal catch.

After a mighty struggle, he managed to catch the fish in the net and drag it out of the water. But as he pulled it in, the salmon took a mighty leap toward the old man, and poor Finnegas fell backward.

Finn MacCool hastily grabbed the fish before it could wriggle back into the pool and gripped it tightly in his giant hands. The battle with the salmon had exhausted old Finnegas. "I need to rest, lad. Cook up the fish for me, and I'll eat it later," he said, then he retreated into his house for a nap.

So, while Finnegas slept, Finn built a great fire and prepared the massive fish. He cooked it slowly on a spit over the flames. It smelled mouth-wateringly good. The fish was almost ready when Finnegas began to stir from his sleep.

"It's nearly done, sir—come and enjoy it," called Finn, and he turned the spit once more. However, just as he did so, the fire sizzled and a drop of piping hot oil from the fish splashed onto his thumb. Without thinking, Finn put his thumb straight into his mouth to ease the burning pain. At that very moment, he felt a rush of knowledge flood his brain, and he was overwhelmed by deep and clever thoughts. His mind felt more alive than ever before!

When old Finnegas saw the brightness in Finn's eyes, he guessed that something had happened. The young giant's expression had completely changed.

"Did you eat some of the fish?" asked Finnegas, unable to hide his frustration.

"No, I swear I didn't," cried Finn.

"Tell me the truth, lad!" demanded Finnegas.

Then, Finn remembered the hot oil burning his skin, and he explained to the old man what had happened. Finnegas sighed—there was nothing he could do now.

"Ah well," he shrugged. "It seems all the wisdom in the world was meant for you and not I, young man." He congratulated Finn and patted him on the back, then they enjoyed a feast of freshly caught salmon.

Finn MacCool, with all the wisdom in the world, no longer needed Finnegas to teach him, so he set off for home and became the bravest hero Ireland ever had—and whenever he needed some wisdom, all he had to do was bite his thumb!

Book Club Questions

1. What are some common elements found in each of the myths and legends?

2. What made each story unique?

3. Many myths and legends explain how certain things in the world came to be. What phenomena could you explain using a myth or a legend?

4. Compare and contrast the character Finn MacCool in "Finn MacCool" and in "The Salmon of Knowledge."

5. How do "The Golden Staff" and "Persephone and the Seasons" portray gods differently?

6. In the "Emperor's Race," why is the cat mentioned at the beginning of the story?